Pizza Party!

by Grace Maccarone

Illustrated by Emily Arnold McCully

Hello Reader!—Level 1

SCHOLASTIC INC.

New York Toronto London Auckland Sydney

We scoop.
We pour.

A NOTE TO PARENTS

Reading Aloud with Your Child

Research shows that reading books aloud is the single most valuable support parents can provide in helping children learn to read.

- Be a ham! The more enthusiasm you display, the more your child will enjoy the book.
- Run your finger underneath the words as you read to signal that the print carries the story.
- Leave time for examining the illustrations more closely; encourage your child to find things in the pictures.
- Invite your youngster to join in whenever there's a repeated phrase in the text.
- Link up events in the book with similar events in your child's life.
- If your child asks a question, stop and answer it. The book can be a means to learning more about your child's thoughts.

Listening to Your Child Read Aloud

The support of your attention and praise is absolutely crucial to your child's continuing efforts to learn to read.

- If your child is learning to read and asks for a word, give it immediately so that the meaning of the story is not interrupted. DO NOT ask your child to sound out the word.
- On the other hand, if your child initiates the act of sounding out, don't intervene.
- If your child is reading along and makes what is called a miscue, listen for the sense of the miscue. If the word "road" is substituted for the word "street," for instance, no meaning is lost. Don't stop the reading for a correction.
- If the miscue makes no sense (for example, "horse" for "house"), ask your child to reread the sentence because you're not sure you understand what's just been read.
- Above all else, enjoy your child's growing command of print and make sure you give lots of praise. *You are your child's first teacher—and the most important one. Praise from you is critical for further risk-taking and learning.*

—Priscilla Lynch
Ph.D., New York University
Educational Consultant

To three men who love to cook
with kids: Nick Keyembe,
David Heckerling, and Salvatore Maccarone
—G.M.

Library of Congress Cataloging-in-Publication Data

Maccarone, Grace.
Pizza party / by Grace Maccarone ; illustrated by Emily Arnold McCully.
p.   cm. — (Hello, reader!)
"Level 1."
Summary: A group of children have fun making a pizza.
ISBN 0-590-47563-0
[1. Pizza—Fiction.   2. Stories in rhyme.]   I. McCully, Emily
Arnold, ill.   II. Title.   III. Series.
PZ8.3.M127Pi   1994
[E]—dc20   93-19732
CIP   AC

Text copyright © 1994 by Grace Maccarone.
Illustrations copyright © 1994 by Emily Arnold McCully.
All rights reserved. Published by Scholastic Inc.
CARTWHEEL BOOKS is a registered trademark of Scholastic Inc.
HELLO READER! is a registered trademark of Scholastic Inc.

2019181716151413   5 6 7 8/9

Printed in the U.S.A.

First Scholastic printing, January 1994

We pour some more.

We fill.
We spill.

We wipe the floor.

We clean.

We fix.

We help to mix.

We push.

We poke.

We roll.

We joke.

We wait awhile.

We play.

We smile.

We pull.

We toss.

We stretch,

add sauce.

We cut.

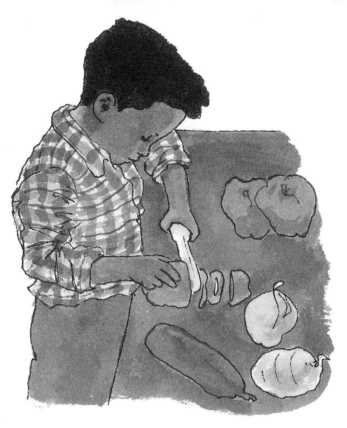

We shred.

We taste.

We spread.

It cooks.
We look.

We read a book.

It's done.
What fun!

We eat our pie.

We're done!
What fun!

We say good-bye!